An I Can Read Book™

# ADVENTURES OF
# SPIDER-MAN

Sandy Creek

This 2010 edition was created exclusively for Sandy Creek
by arrangement with HarperCollins Publishers.

HarperCollins Publishers® and I Can Read Books® are registered trademarks.

ADVENTURES OF SPIDER-MAN

Spider-Man: Spider-Man Versus Electro
© 2009 Marvel Entertainment, LLC, and its subsidiaries.

Spider-Man: Spider-Man Versus Kraven
© 2009 Marvel Entertainment, LLC, and its subsidiaries.

Spider-Man: Spider-Man Versus the Green Goblin
© 2009 Marvel Entertainment, LLC, and its subsidiaries.

Spider-Man: Spider-Man Versus the Lizard
© 2009 Marvel Entertainment, LLC, and its subsidiaries.

Spider-Man: Spider-Man Versus the Vulture
© 2009 Marvel Entertainment, LLC, and its subsidiaries.

MARVEL, all related characters and the distinctive likenesses thereof: TM & © 2009 Marvel
Entertainment, LLC, and its subsidiaries. Licensed by Marvel Characters B.V. www.marvel.com

www.icanread.com

Sandy Creek
387 Park Avenue South
New York, NY 10016

ISBN 978-1-4351-2651-0
Manufactured in China.
Manufactured 04/2012
Lot 12 13 14 15 SCP 10 9 8 7 6

# Spider-Man Versus Electro

## By Susan Hill
## Illustrations by MADA Design, Inc.

## PETER PARKER

Peter Parker lives in New York City.

## FLASH THOMPSON

Peter goes to school with Flash Thompson. Flash isn't always very nice to him.

## ELECTRO

Electro is the newest villain in town. He can control the power of electricity.

## SPIDER-MAN

Peter has a secret identity.
He is Spider-Man!
He can walk on walls and shoot webs.

"Look out, bookworm!"
yelled Flash Thompson.
Flash threw a water balloon.
It hit Peter Parker on the head.

"But I'm not a bully.

I'm Spider-Man,

and I use my powers for good,"

Peter said quietly as he walked.

Suddenly, the giant screen in Times Square lit up.

A horrible face appeared.

"I am Electro,"

boomed a voice from the screen.

"All the power of electricity

is mine!" he said.

"With my electric rays I will put

the entire city in the dark.

Everyone will respect me!

Everyone will know my name!"

"What was that name again?"
said Peter.

"Buzzy? Sparky?"

Electro spoke from his hideout.
"In five minutes,
the city will be dark.
Hospitals, schools, and jails,
all dark!" he said.

Peter knew what he had to do.

He put on his mask and suit.

He became Spider-Man!

"Electro must be at a power plant.

But which one?" said Spider-Man.

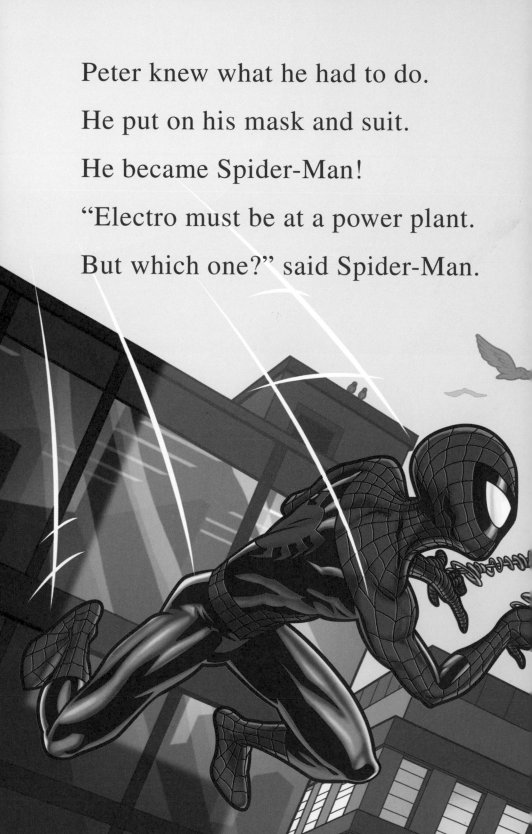

A police helicopter flew over.

"That was easy," said Spider-Man.

"Maybe I could get a ride!"

Spider-Man swung to the helicopter.

He was lifted high over the city.

Suddenly, the helicopter buzzed.

"We've been hit!" yelled the pilot.

"We've lost all power!"

Spider-Man quickly shot webs
to catch the helicopter.
"Thanks, Spider-Man!"
said the pilot.
"Anytime," said Spider-Man.
"But speaking of time,
I've got four minutes
to save the city!"

Spider-Man swung
to the power plant.
Electro was inside.
His body was charging
with electric power.

"Hey, Sparky!" shouted Spider-Man.

Electro turned and shot

a lightning bolt at Spider-Man.

"Don't call me Sparky!" he shouted.

"Missed me!" said Spider-Man.

Spidey hit Electro with a web.

*Pfffft!* The web sizzled to dust.

"Ha!" said Electro.

"Your powers are no good!
One touch of my electricity
and you'll fry!"

Spider-Man knew Electro was right.

How could he stop him?

Electro shot another bolt.

Spider-Man swung out of the way

just in time.

Then Spidey saw something helpful.

"The janitor won't mind if I borrow

his rubber gloves and boots."

The rubber will help protect me

from the electricity!" he said.

With the gloves on,

Spider-Man could knock Electro down.

But Electro shot back up

and sent Spider-Man flying!

"Ouch!" said Spider-Man.

He had crashed into a big pipe.

"Water!" he said.

"Why didn't I think of that?

Everyone knows mixing water

and electricity is very dangerous!"

Electro lifted his hands to shoot

one more bolt.

"Soon the city will be dark

and you'll show me some respect!"

he shouted.

"You don't get respect by being a bully, Sparky!" said Spider-Man.

Spidey turned on the water.

*Woosh!*

"It's lights-out for you, Electro!

Kids, don't try this at home!"

Electro fell to the floor.

"I've done it!" said Spider-Man.

"When Electro wakes up in jail,

it'll be the shock of his life!"

# Spider-Man Versus Kraven

by Susan Hill
pictures by Andie Tong
colors by Jeremy Roberts

## PETER PARKER

Peter Parker is a very
good student.

## MR. JAMESON

Peter works for Mr. Jameson
at the *Daily Bugle*.

## KRAVEN THE HUNTER

Kraven the Hunter is one evil guy
He collects endangered animals,
but not to save them.
He just wants them for himself.

## SPIDER-MAN

Peter has a secret identity.
He is Spider-Man!

"Grab your camera, Parker!"
yelled Mr. Jameson.

"What's up?" Peter Parker asked
his boss at the *Daily Bugle*.

"Another rare animal was stolen
from the zoo!" Mr. Jameson said.

Peter hurried to the zoo.

He saw a strange man

wearing animal skins!

The man unlocked a tiger's cage.

Peter quickly stuck his camera

to the wall with webbing.

Peter changed into his costume.

Peter does not just take pictures.

He also fights crime.

Peter Parker is Spider-Man!

He swung to the cage and locked it.

The tiger was safe!

Then Spidey swung around
and quickly shot a web
to trap the bad guy.

41

"Who are you?" said Spidey.
"And may I give you a ride
to the police station?"

The man laughed.

Then he broke through

Spider-Man's web!

"I'm Kraven the Hunter!"

he yelled.

Spider-Man jumped out of the way as Kraven attacked.

"I am a great hunter," Kraven said. "I have caught hundreds of animals for my collection!"

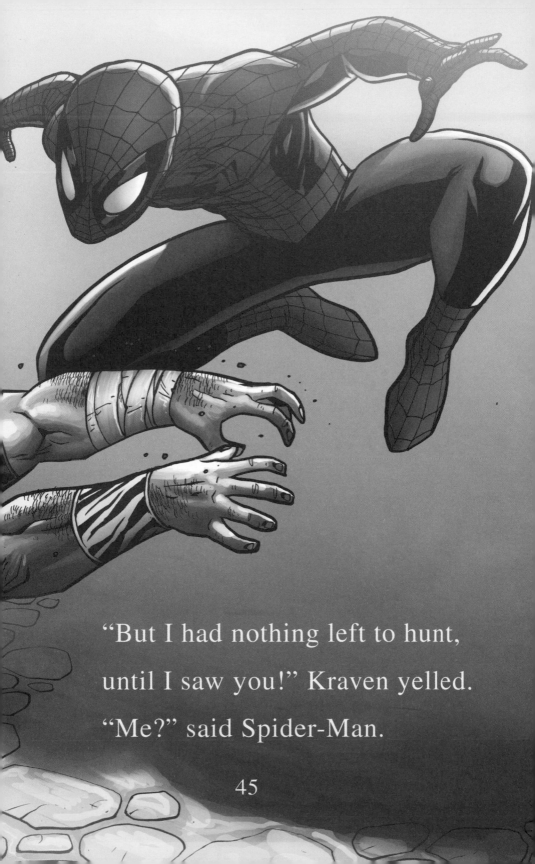

"But I had nothing left to hunt,
until I saw you!" Kraven yelled.
"Me?" said Spider-Man.

45

Kraven grabbed Spider-Man
and held him in a powerful grip.

Quickly, Spider-Man broke free.

He hit Kraven hard.

"Take that, Leopard Pants!"

said Spider-Man.

Kraven leaped out of the way.
"A good hunter always has
a few tricks up his sleeves,"
he said.

Spider-Man jumped on Kraven's back.

"You don't have any sleeves!"

said Spidey.

"I've got you now!"

"No, you don't!" Kraven yelled.

Kraven took out something

small and sharp.

Spider-Man didn't see it.

His spider-sense gave him a warning.

But what was wrong?

As Spider-Man fought,

Kraven scratched him!

Spider-Man fell from Kraven's back.

"What was that?

I feel dizzy," said Spider-Man.

"It was jungle potion," Kraven said.

"It will make you weak

while I plan my next attack!"

"Remember the law of the jungle,"

Kraven said.

"Hunt or be hunted!"

Then he ran away into the night.

The potion kept Spider-Man weak.

His hands shook

and his head hurt.

"I can't fight crime like this,"
Spider-Man said.
"If Kraven finds me,
he'll trap me for his collection."

Then Spider-Man remembered
what Kraven had said.
Hunt or be hunted.
Spidey knew what he had to do.

Spider-Man looked for Kraven

all night long.

At last, his spider-sense

led him to the hunter's hideout.

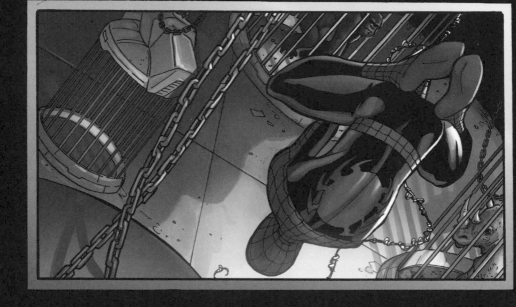

Spider-Man saw the stolen animals and one empty cage.

"That cage will not be for me!" Spider-Man said to himself.

"Too many people need me!"

Suddenly, Spider-Man felt strong!

Spider-Man jumped into the room.

Kraven leaped to his feet.

"It was a mistake for you to come.

Now I will trap you!" Kraven said.

"Just try!" said Spidey.

Spider-Man shot a web
to catch Kraven.

Kraven broke the web and attacked!

But Spider-Man shot another web!

And another!

And another!

This time, the webs held.

Spider-Man felt much better.

He had stopped Kraven

and found the missing animals.

Spider-Man put Kraven in the cage.

He made sure to take some pictures

for the newspaper.

"I'll get you yet!" said Kraven.

"But I must know one thing.

Are you man or beast?"

Peter smiled behind his mask.

"I'm Spider-Man!" he said.

# SPIDER SENSE SPIDER-MAN®

## Spider-Man
## Versus the Green Goblin

by Susan Hill
pictures by Andie Tong
colors by Jeremy Roberts

## PETER PARKER

Peter Parker is
a good student
and a loyal friend.
But he has a secret.

## HARRY OSBORN

Peter's best friend
is Harry Osborn.

## THE GREEN GOBLIN

The Green Goblin
is Spider-Man's
newest enemy.
He has a secret, too!

## SPIDER-MAN

Harry doesn't know Peter's secret. Peter is Spider-Man!

"Harry, why weren't you at school?"
Peter Parker asked his best friend,
Harry Osborn.

"There was an accident at OsCorp, where my father works," said Harry. "Peter, my father was hurt! And now he is missing!"

Peter left Harry's house.

"I promised Harry I'd help find
his father," said Peter.
"I just didn't tell him
I'd help as Spider-Man!"

Spidey swung on a web

toward OsCorp.

But suddenly, he heard a cry.

"Help! Someone help me!"

Spider-Man saw a man

lying on the ground.

He swung down to see what happened.

"It was horrible!" cried the man.

"A creepy green guy

swooped down on a flying glider!

He hit me and stole my money!"

"In my line of work, I see a lot of
creepy green guys,"
said Spider-Man.
"Don't worry, I'll find him."

Spider-Man swung through the city,
looking for the crook.
"I'll find this green guy first.
Then I'll find Mr. Osborn,"
said Spider-Man.

Soon Spidey's spider-sense
led him to the villain.
"There's that green guy now!"
said Spider-Man.
"Hand over the money!"

The green man spun around
and flung the wallet at Spider-Man.
"Keep the change, Web-head!"
he shouted.

"I am the Green Goblin.

With my bag of gadgets,

I will take over the city!" the man yelled.

"What is this, Halloween?" said Spidey.

"Trick or treat!"
shouted the Green Goblin
as he threw pumpkin bombs.
Smoke blew out of them!

"Hey, who turned out
the lights?"
said Spider-Man.
He swung out of the smoke.

82

"The Goblin's smoke bomb could only be made by OsCorp!" Spidey said to himself. "But what does that mean?"

"If you don't like pumpkins,

how about bats?" said the Goblin.

He sent a robot bat flying

at Spidey's face.

It ripped Spider-Man's mask.

"Oh, no!" cried Spidey.

"The Green Goblin can see my face!"

Spider-Man was angry and afraid.

He used the bat's sharp wings

to rip the Goblin's mask, too.

Spidey couldn't believe what he saw.

"Mr. Osborn?" cried Peter.

"How could you be the bad guy?"

"And how could Peter Parker

be a Super Hero?" said Mr. Osborn.

"That's a laugh!"

"It's not funny, Mr. Osborn.

Harry is worried about you!"

said Peter.

"What happened to you?"

"In the accident at OsCorp,

I was turned into the Goblin!"

said Mr. Osborn.

"I have powers I never dreamed of!"

"Don't use your powers for evil,
Mr. Osborn!" said Peter.
"Think of all the good you can do!"

"I'll leave that to you, do-gooder,"
said Mr. Osborn.
Then he pulled another
pumpkin bomb from his bag
and threw it at Spider-Man!

Spidey dove out of the smoke
and tackled the Green Goblin!
The Goblin fell to the ground
and hit his head.

"I must help Mr. Osborn,"
said Spider-Man.
"I promised Harry!"
Spider-Man hid the Goblin costume
and took Mr. Osborn to a hospital.

Later, Peter and Harry went

to the hospital together.

Peter was worried.

Would Mr. Osborn keep Peter's secret?

"Dad!" shouted Harry.

"Harry! Peter!" cried Mr. Osborn.

"What happened, Dad?" said Harry.

Mr. Osborn rubbed his head.

"I must have lost my memory

in the accident at OsCorp,"

said Mr. Osborn.

"The doctors say

Spider-Man saved me!"

"That was close!" said Peter to himself.

"My secret is safe for another day!"

# Spider-Man Versus the Lizard

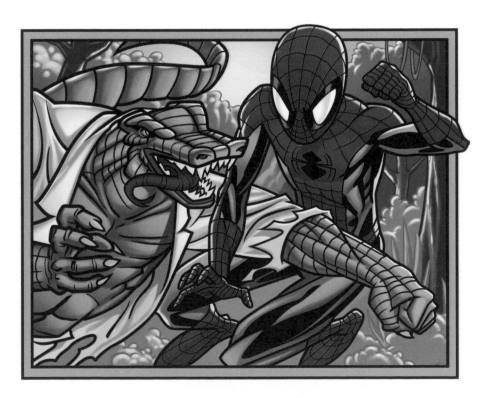

by Susan Hill
pictures by MADA Design, Inc.

## PETER PARKER

Peter is a regular kid,
with a big secret:
He is also Spider-Man!

## MR. JAMESON

Mr. Jameson is Peter's boss.
He wants Peter to take
pictures for his newspaper.

## MRS. CONNORS

Mrs. Connors needs
Spider-Man's help.

## THE LIZARD

Mrs. Connors's husband has
had a terrible accident.
He has turned into the Lizard!

Can Spider-Man find a cure for the Lizard before it's too late?

"Welcome to Florida, Parker,"

Mr. Jameson said.

"Now, get to work!"

"Yes, sir!" said Peter Parker.

"But what is the story?" he asked.

Mr. Jameson wrote on a pad.

"Here's the headline," he said.

Peter read it.

"Monster Lizard Loose in Swamp!"

Peter took his camera to the swamp.

"It's quiet," he said.

Suddenly, Peter heard

a terrible roar.

He leaped into action!

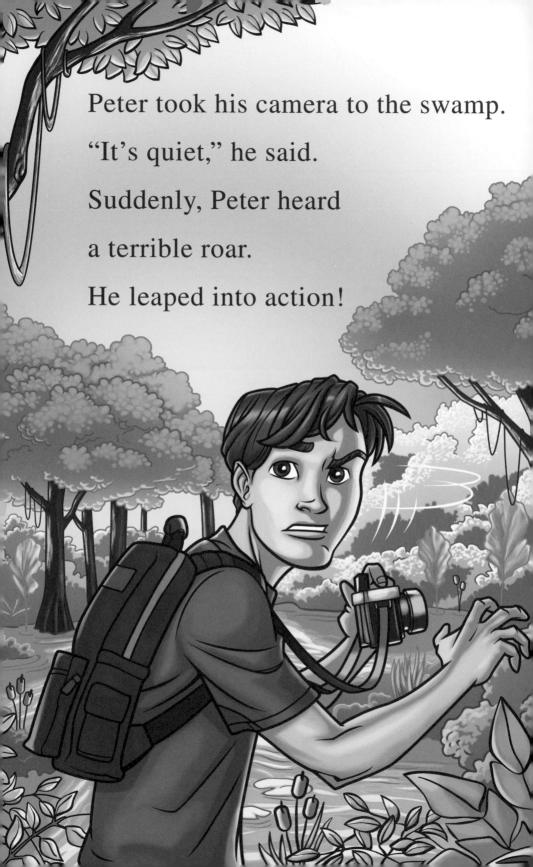

"I may be a skinny kid
on the outside," Peter said
as he put on his mask.
"But I'm also Spider-Man!"

Spider-Man swung toward the sound of the roar.

Then he saw something horrible, big, and green.

"Gee, how did a little lizard
grow up to be a big, green monster
like you?" said Spider-Man.
"And what's with the lab coat?"

The monster roared at Spider-Man.

"I used to be Dr. Curtis Connors,

until I drank this potion.

Now I am the Lizard!"

The Lizard lashed his tail
and knocked Spider-Man down.
"Hey, watch that thing!"
said Spider-Man.

"I am making a giant lizard army,"

said the Lizard.

"I will rule the world!"

"That's a slimy thing to do,"

said Spider-Man.

The Lizard picked up
Spider-Man in his powerful claws
and threw him into the air.

Spider-Man landed in a tree.

"Talk about a crash landing,"
Spider-Man said.

There were big, hungry crocodiles
under the tree.

"Time to floss!" said Spidey.

Spider-Man shot out strong webs
and shut the crocodiles' jaws.

Then Spider-Man saw a house.

The name on the mailbox

was Connors.

Spidey swung down on a web

and knocked on the door.

A woman answered.

She was crying.

She told Spider-Man she was

the wife of Dr. Connors.

"Underneath that lizard skin,
he is still my husband," she said.
"He is Dr. Connors and the Lizard,
in the same body!"

"Dr. Connors is just like me!"

thought Spider-Man.

"I'm a kid and a Super Hero,

in the same body!"

Mrs. Connors showed Spider-Man
her husband's lab.

"This is where he made a potion
to regrow arms and legs
the way lizards can," she said.
"He wanted to help people.
But something went wrong!"

"Dr. Connors is a good man
trapped inside an evil monster
he can't control,"
said Spider-Man.
"I must find a cure!"
Hours later, the cure was ready.
"I've done it!" cried Spider-Man.
"The Lizard must drink it
before it's too late!"

Just then the Lizard came in.

"Perfect timing!" said Spider-Man.

Spidey tried to grab the monster.

But the Lizard slashed his claws

and snapped his jaws.

"That's a cold-blooded thing to do,"
said Spider-Man.

Spidey sprang away and shot a web.
The Lizard broke it with one thrash
of his powerful tail.

The Lizard opened his jaws to roar.

Spider-Man saw his chance.

He poured the cure

down the monster's throat!

The Lizard thrashed

and roared.

"I can't tell if it's working!"

cried Spider-Man.

But suddenly,

the Lizard's skin became flesh.

"I'm human again!" said the doctor.

"And I never got any pictures

for my story," Spidey said quietly.

"Thank you!" said Dr. Connors.

"It's good to be myself again!

It was hard to be

one thing on the outside

and another on the inside!"

"I know,"
said Spider-Man.
"Believe me, I know."

# Spider-Man Versus the Vulture

by Susan Hill
pictures by Andie Tong
colors by Jeremy Roberts

## PETER PARKER

Peter Parker is a very good student.

## FLASH THOMPSON

He goes to school with Flash Thompson.

## AUNT MAY

Peter lives with his aunt May.

## SPIDER-MAN

Peter has a secret identity.
He is Spider-Man!

## MR. JAMESON

Peter works for Mr. Jameson
at the *Daily Bugle*.

## THE VULTURE

The Vulture is one of
Spider-Man's worst enemies.
Can Spidey stop him from
causing danger?

"What's your hurry, Peter?" the teacher asked.

"Today is my first day at the *Daily Bugle*," said Peter. "I can't be late!"

"Too bad you can't swing on a web like Spider-Man!" said the teacher.

"Ha!" Flash Thompson laughed. "Peter Parker, a Super Hero? He's just a bookworm!"

Peter disliked being called names
like bookworm, geek, or nerd.
"If only he knew my secret.
Then I'd show that bully."

Peter was going to be late!

"I know how to get there fast,"

Peter thought.

He ran into an alley

and pulled off his street clothes.

Under Peter's shirt
was a Super Hero costume.
Shy Peter Parker was Spider-Man!

Ever since Peter was bitten

by a super-spider,

he has had superpowers!

He has spider-senses.

He has spider-strength.

And he can climb like a spider!

The Vulture appeared from above.

"What's your hurry, Spider-Man?"

The Vulture was a tricky enemy.

He had wings and could fly.

"Vulture! What are you doing here?"
said Spider-Man.

"Gosh," Spider-Man thought.

"I am so late.

I must get to the *Daily Bugle*."

Then Spidey remembered something.
With great power comes
great responsibility.
He had to stop the Vulture.
But where had the Vulture gone?

The Vulture swooped behind
Spider-Man on silent wings.
One flick of his wing
sent Spider-Man flying off the roof!

145

Spider-Man clung to the wall.

"How does Vulture fly

on silent wings?" he thought.

"I know! Silent magnetic power!"

Spider-Man climbed up the wall
on a web.
"I'm ready for you this time,
Vulture!" said Spider-Man.

Spider-Man took his homemade magnet reverser out of his backpack.

"This is the perfect time
to test my invention," he said.
Spider-Man aimed it at the Vulture.

"What did you do?

I can't fly!" said the Vulture.

150

The Vulture crashed to the ground.

"My invention worked!" said Spidey.

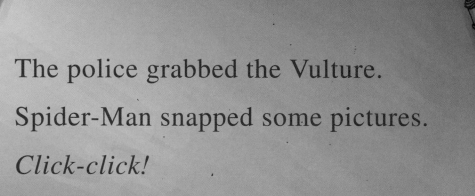

The police grabbed the Vulture.

Spider-Man snapped some pictures.

*Click-click!*

"My new boss will love these photos!"

he said.

Peter put on his street clothes.

He was very late now.

He hurried to the *Daily Bugle*.

The boss, Mr. Jameson, was mad.

"Parker! You're late!" he yelled.

"But wait till you see my photos,"
said Peter.

"How did a shy guy like you get great photos like these?" said Mr. Jameson.

"All in a day's work," Peter said.

Mr. Jameson paid Peter well.

Now Peter could do something nice

for his aunt May.

*Splash!*

"Ha-ha! Sorry, nerd!" said Flash.

"If I used my amazing spider-powers, he really would be sorry!" thought Peter.

But Peter was happy,
even if no one could ever know
his amazing secret.
"I'm not a nerd. I'm Spider-Man!"